The Farmer & Dale

A Guide to Handling Today's Stress

by
Stephen Havertz

BONNEVILLE BOOKS™
Springville, Utah

ISBN: 1-55517-591-0
v.1

Published by Bonneville Books
Imprint of Cedar Fort Inc.
www.cedarfort.com

Distributed by:

Typeset by Kristin Nelson
Cover design by Adam Ford
Cover design © 2001 by Lyle Mortimer

Printed in the United States of America
10 9 8 7 6 5 4 3 2 1

Printed on acid-free paper

Library of Congress Cataloging-in-Publication Data

Havertz, Stephen, 1966-
  The Farmer & Dale : A Guide to Handling Today's Stress / by Stephen Havertz.
    p. cm.
  ISBN 1-55517-591-0 (pbk. : alk. paper)
  1. Stress management--Fiction. I. Title.
  PS3608.A88 F37 2002
  813'.6--dc21

                    2001008091

iv

The Farmer & Dale

A Guide to Handling Today's Stress

Dedication

This book is dedicated to my wife and children for their support through this process of writing and to my parents for their teaching me correct principles in my youth.

Acknowledgments

To all those who read the manuscript
before publication and encouraged me
forward, especially Amy Homer, a colleague
at work.

PREFACE

Everyone has dreams. As a boy while doing chores on his dad's farm, Dale imagined himself in an office, counseling people. He always knew that this was what he wanted to do as a profession. He finally made it through school and started working as a therapist. He was an excellent therapist. His colleagues admired his perseverance with difficult clients. However, many years later some unforeseen circumstances caused him to question his decision to enter the helping profession. An extremely challenging situation sealed his fate, and he decided to leave the profession that he loved.

His life made a full circle as he found himself back on his dad's farm. Tragedy created an unlikely friendship and bond between Dale and his farming neighbor Frank. As a result of this bond, Dale was presently surprised to again be able to use some of his counseling knowledge to help Frank work through some of his most difficult challenges.

As the story progresses, you will notice that Frank and Dale approach stress and difficulties very differently. You will have the opportunity to look at their lives and compare your style of dealing with stress with theirs. See if you can pick out the healthy versus unhealthy coping skills. Some of the stress management tips are very obvious and easy to recognize in the story, while others may take some time and thought to locate and understand. There are many hidden gems of information inside this book. Healthy coping skills used by individuals in this book are summarized and listed on the last page.

In my twelve years of counseling individuals and families, I have found that stories and metaphors were powerful tools that helped create behavioral changes in people. Individuals can abstractly relate to a metaphor, a character in a story, or a story line itself and then come up with their own way to make a positive behavioral change. Many self help books spell out the specific changes they desire of the reader. However, this book gives you the opportunity to see how two individuals, with different personalities, worked through some challenging situations.

The ultimate goal of this book is to allow you to determine, through seeing these two different individuals work through problems, what coping skills may benefit you. Instead of being told what to do and how to do it, I desire that you decide when, how, and what you would like to do to decrease stress in your life. Remember that it is the little things that can make the biggest difference in each of our lives.

INTRODUCTION

The first five to ten minutes after waking were the most difficult for Dale. He always rolled out of bed wishing he could sleep longer. As a boy he enjoyed life on a farm working with his dad, but his aspirations were to become a counselor. Doing chores every morning and bailing hay in the summer were not his favorite activities, but they did not bother him. In fact, there were parts of the farming business that he found appealing. The fresh morning air, the ability to see the results of a hard day's work and the peacefulness of working alone in a huge field provided the needed gratification in his days of youth.

However, he felt he had a knack for being able to understand human behavior. Friends in high school were intrigued with the periodic insights he shared that helped explain the behaviors of troubled individuals. Most adults who knew him commented that he was a level headed, good kid. Mr. Crabtree was the exception. Dale and his friends, whenever they walked by his fenced yard, enjoyed agitating his German Shepherd. One day Mr. Crabtree, caught them shooting water balloons at his dog. Dale had made a bungee-cord-slingshot that shot water balloons about sixty yards. When Mr. Crabtree caught them in the bushes, he promptly began to scold them and threatened to call the police, though he never followed through with the threat.

When Dale graduated from high school he and some

friends took a graduation trip to the majestic Grand Canyon. This was the last meaningful contact he had with his high school buddies. Dale was the most ambitious of all his friends, and a few months after this trip, he registered for his first year of college. Dale was fortunate enough to be able to live at home and work for his father while he attended college.

Dale was so anxious to complete his schooling that he attended summer semesters and completed his Bachelor of Science degree in psychology in three years. He then applied to four different graduate schools and was fortunate enough to be accepted to a counseling program at a university that was about four hours from his home. For two years he lived in a small studio apartment a few miles from campus. He drove a twelve year old Pinto which was on its last piston. While in graduate school, working at his internship, he met his wife. She was the receptionist at the agency where he worked. The first time he saw her, he noticed her big brown eyes. They shone brightly every time she looked at him. She was very friendly and sociable, which offset Dale's reserved personality. His stocky muscular build and olive skin were a contrast to her slender build and fair complexion. They both enjoyed going for walks, movies, pizza, and country music. This was the most exciting time of his life. He had met a wonderful girl and was about to further his child-hood dream. One month after completion of his master's degree, they married, and he began full time employment at another clinic in the area. Emily, his new partner, continued to work at her same job as a receptionist.

Dale had a passion for counseling and it showed in his work. His skills quickly increased as he saw between twenty-five to thirty patients each week. He developed a specialty in family abuse issues. Co-workers, at times, were amazed at his willing-ness to wade through the deep afflictions that plagued the families he counseled. He never gave up on a client.

As the years went by he noticed that the severity of his clients' abuse issues were increasing. Another developing trend was that insurance company benefits and reimbursement rates were decreasing. Trying to work toward resolution of these severe abuse issues, plus the limited insurance benefits available, caused some discouragement and burnout to surface. He noticed that he began to feel more frustrated since he could not help many patients fully resolve their problems, because of their limited insurance benefits.

After about nine years of doing counseling, Dale became increasingly burned out and frustrated. Days seemed to go by more slowly: The work became more taxing emotionally. He found his mind wandering during sessions.

As he began to look around for other job opportunities, a different position came available at the agency where he worked. The position was doing part-time counseling and part-time administrative and staffing work. When he was offered this job, it helped solve his feelings of burnout.

Though the new position went well, a couple of years later he received a subpoena to appear in court for problems regarding a client that he had seen many years earlier. The District Attorney was prosecuting this former patient for some new allegations of sexual abuse. This client was accused of sexually molesting his daughters. The oldest daughter now eighteen years old had recently informed the authorities of the sexual abuse. Dale had to dig up some of the past case notes he had written in this patient's chart. As he recalled from reading his notes, this client admitted to a one-time incident of sexual abuse with one of his daughters. Dale remembered feeling that there was more sexual abuse going on, but sensed that the family was afraid of their dad. He had asked each family member several times in different ways about further abuse, but none was reported. This father finally ended up on probation and was court ordered into therapy.

Dale counseled him individually and used group counseling for about six months. He wrote in the record that he intensely confronted him many times about any other abuse he may have perpetrated, but Dale wrote, "During the confrontations he always calmly denied any abusive actions toward his daughters." However, despite repeated verbal denials, Dale believed that this man either had perpetrated further abuse or would abuse again, but he had no evidence.

The day came for Dale to take the witness stand. Because of confidentiality issues he had to wait for the judge of this case to order his testimony. As a formality the judge ordered Dale to answer questions regarding this case. The District Attorney asked questions concerning the client's treatment and wanted to confirm that the accused had admitted to the sexual abuse of one of his daughter years ago. The questions asked were easily answered. Then came the defense attorney's turn. Dale was completely surprised by the attack on his character and the belittling of his skills as a therapist. It floored him to think that they were holding him responsible for this deviant man's abuse of his own daughters. He knew in his mind that this was a ploy by the attorney to create a lesser sentence for his client, but he was still dismayed by the actions of this defense attorney. After he was humiliated on the stand, he watched the rest of the trial from the back of the courtroom.

A very severe history of sexual abuse was disclosed by this man's ex-wife and oldest daughters. He had even been sexually abusing his daughters during the six months of the psychotherapy that Dale was providing years earlier. The judge was not at all lenient on the sentencing of this abuser. He received the maximum time in prison. This pleased Dale, but still he was troubled.

That evening he was casually watching the evening news, when they showed a video of this man being hauled off to prison. A reporter stuck a microphone near his mouth and asked, "Do you have any comments?" His response really upset Dale. He very sharply and angrily barked, "If Dale Perkins would have provided proper counseling for me, I certainly wouldn't be going to prison." Dale yelled out to his wife, "Did you hear that? He is blaming me for his sick behavior. That doesn't make sense. Why am I the brunt of his anger?"

Dale suddenly felt sick. All the negative feelings of burnout and job stress hit him with such fierce intensity that he raced to the bathroom and threw up. While cleaning himself up, he heard the phone ring, a female voice identified herself as a reporter from a local paper. The reporter asked Emily if her husband was home and would she like to comment on the events of the day. Dale was not feeling well enough to speak to the reporter and told Emily to tell her that he had "no comment."

She took the phone off the hook and went to the bedroom where her husband lay. She sat at the foot of the bed and offered her listening ear. She sat there for many minutes with her hand on his leg. Dale with tears in his eyes turned his head toward Emily and said, "I want out of the counseling business."

Emily groaned and then said, "Honey, you know it's not your fault that those kids were molested."

"I know that in my mind, but there is part of me that wonders if I could have done something different," he said.

Moving toward him on the bed and facing him she said, "Your dad has offered to have us come and build a house on his property and help him run his farm. He is getting old and may eventually let you take over the farm."

A ray of hope entered his body as he lifted his head and said,

"Maybe I'll call my dad and ask him if that is still an option. Then we can discuss it later as a family, but right now I just need some time to think."

A few days later Dale called his dad to explore this option. His dad and mom were saddened by the events relating to his job, but elated at the chance to have Dale, Emily and their grand-children closer. Tentative arrangements were made for them to come and look at a place on the farm where they could build their new home.

Their four children were actually excited about the possi-bility of living on the farm and wanted to know when they could move. So it was decided. Dale gave a month's notice at work which allowed him time to transfer his patients to a new thera-pist. He had several months of vacation time saved up, which helped with the transition to their new place.

It was difficult saying good-bye to his friends and colleagues at work. He had mixed emotions, but knew that it was time to make a change. A couple of weeks before his last day one of his best friends, another psychotherapist, came into Dale's office and closed the door. With a look of concern on his face he ques-tioned Dale about his motives and inquired if he wasn't just running away from his problems.

Dale responded, "I know it may look that way, but I was feeling burned out even before this former client's accusations. This was just the issue that made the decision much easier. I have spent a lot of time thinking about this and feel it's best for me and my family right now."

His friend looked down at the carpet for a moment and said, "I am really going to miss you."

"I will miss you as well. I have enjoyed our friendship," Dale said. "I will also miss helping people, but what I will not miss is the occasional client who wants to justify and rationalize their behavior and blame others for the mess they had created for themselves."

THE NEW PLACE

While their home was being built, Dale and his family lived with his parents. He quickly picked up on the updated equipment and new challenges facing farmers. His dad was overjoyed to have his son at his side. As with any job, there were things Dale enjoyed and parts of farming that were distasteful. He had to get used to waking up earlier than he normally did when doing counseling.

One morning he stepped outside onto the front porch. He took a deep breath of the crisp winter air. Fond memories flooded his mind. He looked around at the barn, the farm equipment, and the mountain range far in the distance. He scanned the borders of some of the land his dad owned. It was so peaceful. The huge tree that hung over the stream on the west part of the property had frost-covered leaves. The sun was just peaking over the horizon in the east, which illuminated a giant patch of fog hugging the ground between the tree and the mountain range. With the backdrop of the mountains ascending above the fog, it looked like a scene from a postcard. It was so beautiful. He wondered why he had not made this move earlier.

Dale's oldest son Todd, who was twelve at the time, was so excited to be on the farm. He was constantly helping out on the farm with chores and with the building of the house. Grandpa was so impressed with Todd's help that he decided to give him one of his horses. Todd was so excited about his new acquisition that he was out in the barn every day taking care of his horse. He was a little timid at first as he learned to ride, but he quickly became secure in letting his horse gallop at a fast pace.

Several months after they got into their new home, Dale and Emily were telling each other how thankful they were that everything was going so smoothly. However, as it is with life, there are always new difficulties that lie in wait.

THE ACCIDENT

No one desires the immediate new perspective that tragedy brings. It can create unseen barriers or divine closeness. It was summertime when the accident occurred. Todd was riding his most prized possession. He kicked his horse, Blackee, in order to get up an embankment. When Blackee was spooked, he reared up and threw Todd to the ground, causing him to land on his head. Frank, the farmer in the next field, saw the accident and ran over to help Todd. When he got close enough, he noticed that Todd was not moving. He knelt beside him not exactly knowing what to do. He had taken a CPR class many years ago, and remembered to feel for a pulse on the neck. He felt all over on the boy's neck, but could not feel any pulsating sensation at all. He panicked and began to scream at the top of his lungs.

Dale had just walked out of the barn when he heard the screams. As he was running toward the scene, he saw the horse standing there and his boy lying on the ground. He had a sick feeling in his stomach. Dale knew he was running, but it was as if everything was moving in slow motion. It seemed as though it took forever to get to his son. He reached Todd and instructed Frank to go call 911. Dale began CPR but it was to no avail. He began to cry bitterly, as he continued to perform CPR. He pleaded with God to let his son live. The ambulance arrived and took over, but the EMT's could not revive Todd. His son was dead. The memories of that day would forever be etched in his mind.

After the funeral Frank and his wife came over to visit. With tears in his eyes Frank began to apologize for not doing enough to help Todd. The grief of losing a son hit Emily again and she began to cry, which caused Dale to cry. After a few moments they all regained composure and Dale softly responded, "Frank, in no way do I hold you responsible for Todd's death. I appreciate that you were so quick to get to where Todd was."

Frank responded, "I remembered from a CPR class a long time ago to feel for a pulse, and when I could not feel one I panicked and started to yell. I am so sorry." Dale and Emily shared with Frank and his wife about how Todd was so obedient and good-natured. They all talked for a few more minutes and when the conversation wound down Frank's wife invited Dale's family over for dinner at their house the following week.

The two families developed a close bond over the next several years. Their children played together, and they periodically would have each other over for dinner and games. Frank was the type of person that was not well organized and at times became easily frustrated. Dale noticed this and periodically tried to help his friend cope more effectively. Frank for the most part let Dale's "psychobabble," as he called it, go in one ear and out the other. Frank joked with Dale and called him a "shrink," but there were times that Frank actually found that Dale's advice made sense.

The time came for a new planting season. Dale had now taken on the full responsibility for his dad's farm. His mom and dad were more interested in retirement. Frank, who had been in the farming business for about seventeen years, had seen some profitable and unprofitable years, but last year was one of the worst yet. Dale also noticed the effects of last year's drought in his wallet. Little did Frank know that Dale would actually help in preparing him for one of the most difficult challenges of his life.

Chapter 1

The First Day of the Planting Season

Frank had been sleeping restlessly for several days because of his concern over the new planting season. He remembered the drought and insect problem of last year, which almost drained their savings. However, they were able to scrape by with some creative budgeting. When he knew that it was time to plant, he slept through his alarm and had to hurry out the door without eating breakfast. He left in such a hurry that he forgot the key to his tractor. Out of frustration, he hit the side of the barn with his fist and started for home. Next, he tripped on the front porch step of his rambler home. He flew forward, and his body crashed into the screen of the front door, breaking out the mesh netting.

"There is another thing I have to fix," he mumbled to himself. He looked down and saw a huge hole in the knee of his overalls. His anger kindled, he grabbed his keys and rushed out to the barn. His barn was still cluttered from the debris of last year's work. He decided to clean up the mess, and while working, he began to crave pancakes. Knowing that he was already behind in his schedule, his clean-up efforts began to drag because he was so hungry. Frank gave in to the hunger pains, and began walking home. While he was walking, his thoughts wandered back to last year's difficulties. The image in his mind of the cracking dry earth discouraged him. This image quickly shifted to a picture of himself as a waiter in town, when he had to supplement his income. When he saw a dried weed lying on the ground, his pace slowed. Again he was reminded of the terrible season last year. Barbara, his wife, heard the door open. When she saw the hole in his overalls and asked, "What happened?"

As if someone just turned on a garden hose, his worries and concerns came spilling out of his mouth. Barbara gently reminded him that although last year was difficult, they were still able to pay their bills. She also in her loving, but firm way, scolded him for giving up after just a half day's work. He acted like he didn't hear her and walked into the bedroom. He flopped down on the bed and continued to ponder all the problems encountered last year, such as the lack of rain and the abundance of crickets. The discouragement he was feeling grew heavier, as these thoughts and memories of last year's problems flashed through his mind. He decided to stay in the house for the rest of the day, because he did not feel like working. He resolved to start again tomorrow.

The next morning he woke up on time and ate breakfast. This time he remembered to get his keys to the tractor. However, as he was using his tiller he noticed the tractor engine was running abnormally. He recalled that he was going to do some maintenance on it during the winter, but had forgotten. He cussed under his breath. As he continued to till, the tractor engine began to sputter and cough. Finally it stopped.

He hit the steering wheel, got off the tractor, kicked the side panel of his fifteen-year-old tractor, and started walking home. He heard Dale's voice calling to him from the next field. "What's the problem?" he yelled.

"My tractor broke down," Frank gruffly replied, and he turned to walk away. While walking he continued muttering under his breath, "What a piece of junk."

As he entered the front door of his house Barbara asked, "What's wrong?"

With a nasty look on his face he loudly responded, "That

junky tractor just quit on me."

"Did you service it like you said you were going to during the winter?" she asked.

"Of course I didn't," he said sarcastically. "Even if I would have serviced it, that piece of junk would have quit on me anyway."

Barbara, now a little frustrated, responded, "Frank, you don't know that. In the past when you had done the proper maintenance, it seemed to run just fine." Frank didn't say anything, but angrily walked past her to the bedroom and shut the door.

Dale's First Day

Although he had mentally prepared himself for this day, his first day of plowing was not much better that Frank's. However, trying to be proactive, he planned to implement a new irrigation strategy that would hopefully help keep the crops watered. He also planned to try a new pesticide that he heard about to help minimize insect damage.

He looked forward to this new season with hope and optimism—there were several new changes he would implement. He chose to focus on the potential of the future. When thoughts of the past problems crept into his mind, he acknowledged these struggles but pushed those fears and worries away by reminding himself of his new plan for the future that would combat these past problems.

The new season caused some apprehension, but also Dale's waiting for the day to go into the field was like the anticipation of Christmas day. Carefully, he went over his plans for the day. He had made a list of all the tools he needed to pick up in the barn. He ate his favorite breakfast—pancakes and bacon. He savored each bite. With a smile on his face, he inserted his Walkman earphones in his ears. He pressed play on his tape player, and a song by his favorite singer Faith Hill blasted in his ears. He walked out his front door, leaped down the front steps and hurried out into the field. He was ready to take on the day and the new season.

That afternoon he was paying attention to singing along with Faith Hill when he accidentally ran over a large rock that jammed his tiller. He ripped the headphones out of his ears, turned off the tractor and quickly jumped down to survey the damage.

"Way to go, Dale," he muttered in disgust. He saw that the rock was still jammed in the tiller. He tried to pry it out with a metal bar, but the rock was lodged in tightly. Dale pried for about twenty minutes. Sweat dripped down his face, and his shirt was moist with perspiration. He felt the simmering surges of emotions surfacing like volcano lava ready to spew.

With the metal bar in his hand, he stood up and cocked his arm back as if to throw this crow bar as far as he could out into the field. He took a deep breath, set the crow bar down, and decided to take a break for a few minutes. He realized that his frustration was about to lead to anger and irrational behavior.

He sat down on the tractor and pulled out an apple which he had packed for himself. He enjoyed the sweetness of the fruit while he looked at the beautiful clouds overhead. After he relaxed for a few minutes, he went back to the task at hand. He walked around the tractor and noticed that he could obtain more leverage if he were to get behind the tiller. After a few minutes of effort, this was successful. He tilled for another couple of hours and decided to quit for the day.

Walking home, he turned around and spent a few minutes admiring his accomplishments of that day. He realized that he was a little behind schedule, but was confident he could make it up tomorrow. Overall he was happy with his first day's work. He was very thankful he was able to get the rock out of his tractor tiller.

Chapter 2

The Hailstorm

One day early in the season a severe storm alert was broadcast on the news. Some of the crops were just starting to come up out of the ground. It had rained all night and when both farmers awoke it was still raining. They both fed their animals, but decided to stay indoors until the storm subsided. However, that afternoon both were faced with the potential devastation of a hailstorm.

Frank's Hail

Frank was in watching television, when he heard the sound of hail on his roof. He ran to the window, looked out at his crops, and began to pace back and forth between the kitchen table and the window. Barbara noticed his concern and said, "Dear it will be all right." As soon as she made the comment, she knew she had said something wrong.

His face wrinkled up in anger and he snapped back at her, "You don't know that, and anyway why is that your answer for everything?" A little taken back by his behavior, she turned around and went back to doing the dishes. She realized that if she said anything further it would start a fight. Frank waited for a response from his wife. When she did not offer one he turned and walked out onto the porch and again checked on the storm. He noticed his kids being dropped off by the school bus in his driveway.

As they came up to the porch, dodging the hail, in unison they said, "Hi Daddy! How's it going?"

He mumbled back, "This hail is ruining my crops."

His little ten-year-old girl with her pleading blue eyes and sweet voice said, "Daddy can you come and help me with my homework?"

A little irritated he yelled, "Didn't you hear me? This hail is ruining my crops!" He turned and again started pacing. His little girl looked over at her mom, who was watching from the kitchen. Barbara beckoned her, with a hand motion, to come over toward her.

"Dad's a little stressed today. We'd better just leave him alone," she whispered in her ear.

When the hail subsided, he walked outside to inspect the damage to his tender crops. There was definitely some damage, but it was difficult to tell exactly how much. He knew that some of the crops would bounce back, and some would die. As he walked back to the house, his mind was drawn back to some of the previous bad years. He grumbled out loud, "Why me? I am going to have another bad year, I just know it. I can't believe it! I'll probably have to sell the farm." He entered the house and continued his negativity to his wife.

Barbara quickly interrupted his ranting and with conviction responded, "Frank we have been through tough times before, and we will make it again." Frank knew his wife was right, although he had been hoping for some sympathy.

"You don't understand. We are not going to be able to pay our bills," he said in a whiny voice.

Barbara took Frank's hand and softly said, "Frank, it seems that whenever a difficulty arises you immediately jump to the worst conclusions that can occur and convince yourself that these terrible things are going to happen. I just want you to know that I believe in you and know that we can make it." Frank, still not convinced, sat down on the couch and stared mindlessly at the TV. A few minutes later his kids came down stairs.

Trying to cheer him up they surrounded their dad and excitedly said, "Come on Dad let's have a family Nintendo championship."

Frank got up off the couch, looking very dejected. "No, I've got things to do," he said, and walked to his bedroom.

Over the next few weeks Frank's continued inspection of the crops revealed that the damage was not as significant as he expected. However, his focus was still centered on the crops that died. He was still irritable and distant from his family.

Dale's Hail

As the hail started to fall, Dale initially panicked and ran outside thinking he could save some of his crops. The falling hail stung his body as it hit his bare arms and head. The constant pricking quickly brought him back to reality. Recognizing that it was out of his control, he turned around and quickly headed toward the front door of his house. Once he made it to the porch, he looked over his shoulder at the falling hail and let out a big sigh. He wondered how devastating this storm would be. He decided to go to his bedroom and kneel down to pray. Dale asked God to protect his crops. He also prayed that the damage would be minimal. His wife saw his concern and softly whispered, "It will be okay, honey."

Dale, with worry very apparent in his voice responded, "I certainly hope so."

It was difficult for Dale to just sit and wait out the storm.

He found himself pacing between the kitchen table and the window, his heart beating faster than normal because of the anxiety he was experiencing. Finally he thought of the "Serenity Prayer."

"God grant me the serenity to accept the things I can not change, the courage to change the things I can, and the wisdom to know the difference."

He reminded himself that he would have to accept the fact that this storm was something he could not change. Though he sat down and tried to read, he was continually bombarded with the intrusive negative thoughts about his crops being damaged. He had to keep reminding himself of the "Serenity Prayer" in order to reduce the anxiety.

His children arrived home from school and noisily came through the front door. Dale's ten-year-old girl asked for help with her homework. He decided that this would be a good way to occupy his mind with something other than his worries about his crops and the storm. While helping his daughter, his thoughts still went back and forth between his worries and her homework. He pondered the worst case scenario of having to sell the farm or of doing many extra odd jobs in order to survive financially. The thought of having to do counseling again to make some extra money distressed him. However, he quickly remembered that he and his wife had been successful at budgeting through difficulties in the past. He found some comfort from these thoughts.

In his thoughts he remembered a particular client who worried about everything. Every day this patient worried that she might get into an auto accident, worried that her kids would fail school, and worried that her husband would lose his job. Her worries continued on and on. Dale recalled challenging her to list on paper all of her worries. He then worked with her on recognizing that 99 percent of her worries never occurred. With each worry he also asked her to also come up with the absolute worst case scenario that could happen. With each scenario, he asked her if that worst case scenario actually occurred and did she think she could handle it? She soon realized that if she could handle this worst case scenario, she could handle any other problem that was less severe. She also learned from her written log that 99 percent of her worries never happened. Dale contemplated the good work he did with her, and knew he needed to take his own advice.

His daughter's question about a particular story problem brought his mind back to the task at hand. He helped her complete her homework and asked the other children if their homework was done, and then said to his kids, "Let's go see who can make the most colorful chocolate sundae in the kitchen." They all cheered as they raced to the freezer to pull out the ice cream.

A few weeks later, while inspecting the damage from the hailstorm, he became very grateful that the damage was not as bad as he had anticipated. He silently prayed and thanked God for answering his earlier prayer. He realized that things could have been much worse, and in his daily prayers he continued thanking God that most of his crops survived.

Chapter 3

The Build Up

Weeks went by and Frank's problems began to climax. He was behind in his farm work. His eight-year-old was having some behavioral problems in school, and he was trying to serve as the Scout Leader. He became more irritable, and the littlest things caused him to snap at people. The other day, while in the check-out line at the grocery store, he did something that was totally out of character for him. When the woman in front of him began having a long conversation with the checker about which brand of panty hose to buy, Frank yelled out, "Come on, don't you know that people here are in a hurry?" He said it so loudly that all the people at the front of the store turned and looked at him. After he bought his groceries he hurried and left the store feeling more stressed.

His children periodically asked, "Dad are you all right?"

He just responded by mumbling under his breath, "Yeah, no problem here." His wife almost wished that he would not come home at night because he was so grumpy. He was slower and less productive on the farm. Although he was tired, still he could not sleep very well at night. While he was out working during the day, little problems kept him from accomplishing his goals. To make things worse he noticed grasshoppers eating some of his crops. This was the last straw and he "lost it." He wildly ran to his tractor and grabbed a four-foot length of plastic sprinkler pipe and as fast as he could started trying to whack all of the little critters. Every time he saw one he hit the ground with his pipe several times, each time missing his target. Initially, this caused more anger, which fueled his resolve to squash each and every last insect. He began to tire out, and his ability to "whack" slowed. In the back of his mind he knew it was a waste of time and effort, but he continued whacking. It was quite a sight for Dale, who watched from his tractor in the next field. Dirt and crops were flying everywhere. Frank was spinning around and around.

Dale began to laugh at first, but when his friend's behavior continued for several more minutes he became concerned. Dale got off his tractor and started walking over toward his friend, when he noticed that his friend had fallen to the ground. Dale's pace quickened to a run. It looked like Frank was crying.

Dale reached his friend, knelt down, and put his hand on his back and inquired, "Frank, are you all right?"

Frank, with his shirt sleeve, wiped the tears away from his face and with a shaky voice answered, "I'm fine. It has just been a bad day." Dale helped his friend up and suggested that he call it a day. Frank was still breathing heavily and looked a little dizzy when he finally responded, "Yeah, I think I have had enough for today."

Dale walked with his friend to the edge of his front steps. Dale again pressed, "Frank are you sure you're okay?"

Frank responded, "I just need to get some rest."

DALE'S PRESSURES

The pressures were also mounting for Dale. The stress had been increasing because he had been working some extra hours in the evenings, doing backhoe work to help pay for dental bills which they had recently accrued. About this time each year he found himself missing his son who had died four years earlier. The pain of losing his son always caused loneliness and heartache. He recognized that he was becoming more irritable because of the daily stress and memories of the loss of his dear son, and he knew that he needed to do something to decrease his irritations. He recalled from past experiences that he could become very grumpy and petulant. The next day he planned to go fishing after work. Fishing was an activity that relaxed him. He enjoyed the solace it provided. The rest of the day went by more quickly, because he knew that he had something enjoyable to do after work.

He didn't catch anything while fishing, but he went home that evening refreshed. He decided that the next weekend he would take his eight-year-old son Matthew with him to the same fishing hole. Just knowing he had something enjoyable and relaxing to look forward to helped him get through the week.

Help for Frank

The following week, wanting to help his friend, Dale remembered an article about stress that he frequently gave to his patients when he was doing counseling. Hurriedly, he shuffled through various files in the house. He found the article entitled, "Your Stress Tank." Excitedly, Dale slipped out the door with the magazine in his hand and wound his way down the dirt road to Frank's house.

It was a beautiful evening, and while he walked, Dale took a deep breath and allowed the summer aromas in the air to fill his lungs. He slowed his step just slightly so he could take everything in. The shadows that were cast by the setting sun created vibrant contrasts and colors. The depth this created in the trees was marvelous. "This is one of those days when it is good to be alive," he thought to himself.

He knocked on the door of his friend's house, and Barbara, Frank's wife answered. She was wearing jeans and a loose fitting T-shirt. It looked as if she were losing weight. Her brown shoulder-length hair was pulled up in a clip. Her otherwise pretty olive skin showed some slight wrinkles around her eyes and mouth, and there were also some dark circles under her eyes. She did not seem stressed, but her physical appearance seemed to prove his assumption.

Cheerfully, she invited him in, before he could even ask to speak with Frank. Looking very worn out, Frank came into the front room. Dale with his best salesmanship started telling Frank about the article and how he thought it would help him. Frank, half-listening, politely took the papers and thanked his friend. Barbara, who was listening from the other room, took some interest in what Dale had to say and called out, "I think I would like to read it also."

Dale called back, "Oh you will love it. The things in here have helped many people." The three of them talked for a few more minutes and then called it a night.

Barbara took the magazine from her husband, sat down on the couch and started to read. As she patted the cushion on the couch, she commented, "Frank, please sit down here, and I will read it to you." He agreed and let his tired body fall onto the couch, and she began to read.

"YOUR STRESS TANK"

To help conceptualize the impact of stress and quantify your level of stress you have to understand that each of us has what is called a stress tank. Your stress tank holds all of your stress you experience on a daily basis. Stress can come in your tank and leave your tank. Some individuals have a large stress tank and others' tanks are small. The level of stress inside the tank can rise very quickly or slowly depending on the stress you experience on a daily basis. Stress, which is defined as any demand or pressure placed upon us, can come from a **person**, an **event**, or a **choice** we make.

Your perceptions and thoughts can make stress easier or more difficult to deal with, which ultimately means your thoughts can make or break any stressful situation.

A PERSON THAT CREATES STRESS

A person that places stress on you could be a child that is being rebellious, a boss who asks you to complete a project, a spouse who is an alcoholic, or anyone who does or says something that creates demand or pressure.

AN EVENT THAT CREATES STRESS

An event that would create stress would typically be something that is out of your control. A natural disaster, sickness, accident, or things that just happen that you could not have predicted are examples of events that would cause stress.

A CHOICE THAT CREATES STRESS

Choosing to buy a boat that puts you in debt, choosing to be angry, choosing to do something that goes against the values you hold, or choosing to do or say anything that creates demand or pressure on you are examples of choices that cause stress.

You can choose to filter stress out of your tank, but you are not always able to stop stress from entering your tank. The reason for this is that you cannot control the stress that someone else may place upon you, or an unforeseen event that may occur. However you can choose and change how you think and act in relation to these situations.

It is not always best to filter stress out of your tank. You need a certain amount of stress in your tank in order to keep you functioning. In fact, not all stress is bad. People who are in high stress jobs may not want to filter as much stress out while working in order to enable them to perform at their peak level. EMT's, emergency room workers, performers, athletes, and crisis workers are just a few examples of people who may need to keep enough stress in their tank to enable them to perform at their peak level of functioning. **The trick is for us individually to learn how much is too little or too much**.

Generally, it is best to keep your tank level between one fourth and one half full. This leaves you enough room to recognize that the stress level in your tank may be rising, and for you to do something to stop your stress tank from filling further. If your tank level typically rises quickly then you will want to keep less stress in your stress tank and be more aware of the "triggers" that cause your stress tank level to rise. "Triggers" are those events that consistently seem to cause your stress level to rise. For example, if you become stressed every time a bill comes in the mail, then you will need to come up with different more healthy ways to deal with that situation. (Coping strategies will be discussed later.)

KNOW WHAT THE WARNING SIGNS ARE THAT INDICATE YOUR STRESS TANK LEVEL IS RISING

Everyone's warning signs that indicate stress has or is occurring may be different. It is vital that you recognize your own warning signs. **Not only is it important to understand your overall warning signs, but also it is imperative that you know what the earliest warning signs are that indicate your stress tank level is starting to rise. This is the most proactive way to deal with stress. In fact, this is the key to stress management and reduction. All that this takes is a little thought and some self-observation.**

Symptoms can be manifested behaviorally or physically. Below are just a few of the symptoms that you may experience.

Behavioral symptoms would include: crying, acting out, yelling, sitting around, venting, irritability, pacing, performing any type of violence, fidgeting, allowing your leg to "jack hammer," (when someone is sitting still but their leg is pumping up and down like a jack hammer), increasing or decreasing in sleep, appetite, or fingernail biting, self isolation, forgetfulness, etc.

Physical symptoms would include: upset stomach,

vomiting, sweaty palms or feet, cold hands or feat, increased heart rate, shortness of breath, dizziness, hair loss, tense and tight muscles, high blood pressure, headaches, fatigue, etc.

Your whole objective is to monitor your stress tank level. You may accomplish this by knowing the signs, symptoms and "triggers" which indicate your stress tank level has increased or is increasing. Once you understand this you can move on to the second phase, which is learning how to lower your stress tank level. This will be discussed in the next month's magazine. For now, just start monitoring your stress tank level and notice what signs and symptoms develop when your stress tank level begins to rise.

When Barbara finished reading the article, she squeezed Frank's leg with her hand and said, "That seems easy enough."

Frank, trying to act like he didn't find the article that helpful, answered, "Yeah, kind of interesting. I am going to go to bed now."

While he was walking away, she called out, "Frank please tell Dale, when you see him again, to get me the follow-up article."

Chapter 4

Can Good Come From Bad?

The days went by and little problems continued to occur. Frank's five-year-old seemed to spill juice or milk every time they sat down at the dinner table. The kitchen sink dripped and needed a new washer. The clothes dryer only worked some of the time. The children always had problems and questions about their homework. Along with all of his other responsibilities on the farm, his thoughts were focused on the problems and difficulties in his life. He allowed himself to focus mainly on the challenges and struggles. At times he perceived life as a burden which seemed too difficult. It felt as though he were constantly fighting feelings of despair and discouragement.

One day, both farmers were out working toward the back of their property. Dale called out to Frank, "Are things any better for you?" Frank surprised himself, as everything just came spilling out of his mouth. It was as if he could not even stop the flow of words. He told his friend about all the problems that were occurring, and all the projects he had to complete around the house.

Dale responded, "Wow, that is a real load you are carrying."

Dale was about to continue but Frank interrupted his next sentence, "Nothing is going right in my life. . ."

Frank began talking in circles and started repeating himself. Dale waited for a break in Frank's rambling and responded, "I have been there before and it is not fun. When I get that way, I just need to get away. I went fishing with my son last weekend, and that really seemed to help."

"I don't think anything will help me right now," Frank replied.

"That sounds pretty bad, Frank," Dale said. He then asked his friend, "Can you think of anything that is going well or things you are thankful for?"

Frank, a little upset by Dale's question, moved closer to his friend and in a confrontational posture said, "What do you mean? I am up to my ears in problems," waving his hand above his head to gesture that he was buried in problems.

"I know how you feel, but I am just wondering if there is something you can think of that is good in your life?" Dale asked. "Have you been free from accidents and illness lately?"

Frank a little curious about where Dale was going with this statement hesitantly said, "Well, yes."

"Do you have some crops that are doing better than others?" Dale pressed.

"Well, yes," responded Frank. "My corn seems to be doing very well."

"Are your kids flunking out of school?"

"Well, you know my one son has some behavioral problems, and he is struggling in school. In fact, the other day he failed one of his tests. I was really mad at him, because we had gone over his test stuff all night long."

Dale knew that Frank was again starting to ramble so he interjected, "What about the other three? How are they doing?"

"They seem to be doing fine. Hey, what is your point any way?" Frank asked.

Dale patiently said, "I am just saying that we all have various difficulties. I can see that you are up to your ears in problems, but you need to give your mind a break from thinking about just the problems in your life. If you don't take that break, then these issues will consume your thinking. That is when you will only see what is wrong in your world and can not see what is right. If you do not force yourself out of this mode, then you can continue to spiral downward. This may cause you to feel like your life is out of control."

When Frank did not answer, Dale added, "When I get this way I notice I have become reactive to life's problems and not proactive. I have also noticed in myself that I can almost begin to feel sorry for myself. It is a difficult cycle to break, but you have to choose to begin to try to notice the things that you are grateful for and focus on things that are going well. This will give your mind a positive focal point, and it gives you the opportunity to take back control of your life."

CAN ANYTHING GOOD RESULT FROM A BAD SITUATION?

As this dialogue continued, Dale said, "I have also noticed that we can gain strength and confidence from these challenging experiences. It is difficult going through them, but when we have made it through we can find growth and knowledge we can utilize the next time similar problems occur."

Dale asked his friend to think back to a previous time when things seemed to be falling apart. He coaxed him into remembering how things eventually calmed down and worked out. Frank sarcastically responded, "Well of course things eventually calmed down."

"Ok, there is the first thread of courage you can take. You

know from past experiences that things in the past have improved, and it is likely that things can also improve this time. Sometimes this is the only shred of hope we can hang on to.

"Finally, the next challenging step is to discover how these problems may actually benefit you. What did you learn from these problems, so you can apply them to future problems, and in what ways are you stronger as a result of these problems? Second, you learn that time is actually a healer. As the saying goes, time does heal wounds."

Dale further said, "It is many times a matter of what you choose to see and how you choose to perceive it. Let me tell you a story.

"There were two little brothers, one was an optimist and the other was a pessimist. Christmas was coming around the corner and the optimist had been a very bad little boy. However, the pessimist had been a good little boy. The parents decided to reward him with some nice toys for Christmas, and they gave the optimist a big pile of horse manure. On Christmas morning the pessimist saw all of his toys and became depressed and would not play with them. His parents asked what is wrong. He replied, 'If I play with them they will just eventually break anyway so I'm not going to play with them.' Then the parents looked out the window and saw their little optimist digging in the pile of manure, and he was very happy. They asked him, 'What in the world are you doing?' He replied, 'I know that with this much manure there has got to be a horse in here somewhere.'

"You can see," continued Dale, "that our perceptions can make or break many situations. We all need to look for the good even during or after stressful situations. We can find something positive related to almost everything."

"You are telling me to do things that are very difficult,"

Frank said looking very pensive.

"It takes some practice and some conscious effort, but it is well worth it," responded Dale.

When Frank did not respond, Dale continued, "It is very similar to your investment of time, effort, and money which you put into your farm each year. The investment turns out to be worth it in the end. The reason we invest our time, effort and money is because we believe it will benefit us at the end of the year. We do not see a quick return on our investment, but the fruits of our labors are rewarded after months of hard work. If you invest your time and efforts in applying some of these principles, your investment will pay off. You will potentially be happier, less stressed, and feel better physically."

Frank looked down at the ground and said, "You certainly have a conviction of this."

"Well, I know that it will help, if you try it," Dale said.

As they parted that day, Dale was hopeful that he had planted a seed that would be cultivated later by his friend.

Chapter 5

Finding Balance and Priorities

A month had gone by and Frank was really trying to apply some of these principles. He was watching his stress tank level, and he found himself thinking, while he worked, of the potential good that could come out of various problematic situations that had been occurring. A week ago his car had broken down while he was driving his little girl to a friend's house. The car had to be towed to the mechanics' shop. It took a couple of days to be fixed. He noticed that his family actually pulled together and worked out rides with friends and volunteered to walk some places. As he reflected back he caught himself muttering out loud, "As I was calmer my kids were calmer."

It became very clear to him, as if a light had gone on, that his words and actions had had a significant impact on his family.

Although this was a bad situation, he was able to focus on how well the children were responding, instead of focusing on the car problem and how much money it would take to fix it.

However, as life became hectic again he began spending more time working out in the field. The work on the farm became his main activity. He felt as if the kids were being more demanding, and his wife needed more attention. He could not deal with it, and his tendency was to focus most of his time and effort on his work on the farm. His life had become out of balance.

Late one evening Dale saw Frank at the grocery store. Frank softly said, "Hey Dale, what are you buying here this late?"

Dale lifted up some cough medicine and said, "Got a sick kid at home. What are you doing here so late?"

"Oh I'm just looking around," Frank answered as he picked up a bottle of Tylenol, and pretended to be reading the label.

Dale knew there was something wrong and wanted to help Frank, so he said, "I've noticed that you have been working late over the last several weeks."

Frank responded without looking up. "To tell you the truth, as you would call it, my stress tank is almost full. I have been finding more and more projects to do and have been really busy. I wanted to be alone tonight, so I came to the store. You seem to have all the answers. What is wrong with me?" Frank's tone was somewhat sarcastic, but he looked up at his friend intently as if he really wanted an answer.

"It comes back to your stress tank level," Dale said. "You need to find a way to lower it. Your stress can increase as your life becomes out of balance. If someone were to ask you in general what your priorities are, how would you respond?"

Frank quickly said, "My wife and kids are my number one priority."

Dale compassionately confronted Frank, "But your actions are not reflecting this. Your actions show that work is your priority."

Frank angrily responded, "Now wait a minute, the only reason I work is for them. I work so my wife and kids can have the things they need to sustain them."

"You are right, but the only reason you are working so many extra hours is for yourself. This has become your escape from the pressures of life. The priorities you say you have are not being represented by your actions. This happens to all of us at

26

certain times in our lives. We just need to remind ourselves what our priorities are and remember to make sure an appropriate amount of time is spent in relation to each priority."

Frank remained quiet, so Dale continued, "This does not mean that the hours of our day are going to be spent proportionately to each of our priorities. We need to invest some time back into our top priorities. For example, taking an hour out of our week to have a family activity can be all that is needed. It is the little things that make the biggest difference."

Dale further commented, "I have learned some things about keeping life in balance. There are six basic areas that need to be considered when trying to keep things in balance. The categories are social, financial, emotional, educational, physical and spiritual."

Frank jumped in and said, "That sounds like too much to deal with."

"It is really quite easy. You do it most of the time anyway," Dale replied. "It is just a matter of doing it when things are not going well. All you need to do is find an activity you enjoy in one of these areas and start doing it, then add another activity when you feel comfortable.

"When I was doing counseling, I would tell clients about these six areas. If it's all right I'll quickly share with you these things.

Frank looked at his watch and said, "Yeah, I guess it's all right."

SOCIAL

You see, for the social aspect we all need social contact and support. In a sense all of us to one degree or another need to communicate with other human beings. We need someone to listen to us and support us in our trials. We need to have loved ones who will share our joy and pain with us. This social contact gives us strength. Many times just being with our family can be all that is necessary to fill this void.

FINANCIAL

Managing our money means that we need to live within our means. We need to remember that the basic necessities of life are food, water and shelter. Budgeting our money wisely, planing ahead for retirement, children's education, and potential problems are essential.

EMOTIONAL

Managing the emotional aspects of our life means that we basically are watching our stress tank level. We need to keep in check our emotional responses to life's stressful events. We also need to keep our emotions in check by watching our negative thoughts and not allowing them to become out of control.

EDUCATIONAL

We need to be aware that learning is a lifelong process. We learn new things either through life experiences, work, schooling, or self-learning tools. We can never allow ourselves to think we have learned it all.

PHYSICAL

For our physical health, we should manage our hygiene, our diet, and keep up on some sort of physical activities. Our physical bodies and our health are special gifts, and we need to treat them as such. We need to take care of our bodies.

SPIRITUAL

To grow spiritually, we must try to strive for peace within ourselves and adhere to the values and ideals we espouse. The religion we subscribe to is not the issue. What does matter is that we are following our belief systems and that we are trying to make the world a better place.

When stress occurs we sometimes begin to focus too much on one or several areas. We need to see where we are out of balance and make slight adjustments to correct it."

Frank looked more stressed after hearing all of this. Dale recognized his confusion and said, "Just pick one enjoyable thing that you want to do this week and make some time to do it. What would you enjoy doing?"

Frank sneered at Dale slightly and said, "What? I have to pick something and tell you?"

"No, you don't have to do anything you don't want to."

"Well," Frank said, "I'll think about it."

Not wanting to irritate Frank, Dale quickly said, "Sounds good, I better get home to my family."

Frank reciprocated. "I guess I'd better get going also." They both walked up to the cashier, purchased their items, and walked in silence out of the store together.

Chapter 6

Solution Focused Stress Reduction

One day Dale, while out working, looked back at his dad's house and noticed that there was a section of shingles that had been blown off in the last windstorm. He sighed as he thought about the effort it would take to fix that problem. He started pondering his options of whether to try to fix it himself or to hire someone. Both he and his dad's budget were tight, so he decided to fix it himself. When he climbed up on the roof and examined the problem, he quickly realized there was a section of wood underneath the shingles where the tarpaper was gone, and the wood was rotting. In the back of his mind he realized that this problem was quickly developing into something that was a little out of his league. However, he was still determined to try and solve the problem on his own in order to save money. He went to the local hardware store, picked up the supplies, got his tools ready, and started his work. As he cut a hole in the roof he noticed that some of the trusses below the plywood were also rotting. He hit the roof with his fist and let out a muffled scream. Realizing that this was becoming a very serious problem, he sat down to think. Sitting for a few minutes allowed him to regain his determination to conquer this problem. He started cutting a larger section out of his roof. In the back of his mind he realized he was creating a larger problem, but he continued forging ahead. Finally, Dale said to himself, "Here I am cutting a larger hole in my roof knowingly perpetuating the problem. I have got to get some help."

He climbed down from the roof, got on the phone, and called his friend. "Frank," he said, "I know that in the past you have done some roofing. Can you look at my Dad's roof and give me some suggestions on what I need to do to fix it?" Frank came over, climbed on the roof and began his examination. Dale noticed that Frank had a smile on his face while he examined this hole on top of his dad's roof. Dale asked Frank, "What are you smiling about?"

Frank erased the smile from his face and in a serious tone said, "You need some real experts to come out and look at this. I am just glad to see it is not just me that has all of the problems."

Dale responded, "I hope you don't actually believe that?"

"I don't know, it just feels that way sometimes," Frank commented.

Dale said, "Well after today you can hopefully realize that everyone has problems, and this one will be an expensive one for me."

The next day Dale called several places and got some experts to come out and give him some bids.

After his roof was fixed he looked back on the events of the last several days and recognized that one of his weaknesses was trying to save money at any cost. He could have saved himself a great deal of time and suffering if he would have listened to his instincts. Dale had already accepted the fact that he would have to do some extra back-hoeing jobs to pay for the roof.

A few days later Barbara inquired if Frank had ever received the second part of the article on stress management from Dale. Frank, trying to cover up his guilt about not doing what his wife had asked, responded in a forceful tone, "I don't have time to read that."

Barbara read through her husband's ploy to cover up his guilt, and playfully said, "Oh come on, we can take a few minutes tonight and read it together. I'll call Dale, if you go over and get it." Before he could say no, she was dialing Dale's number. Frank heard her say, "No you don't have to bring it over." She hung up the phone and said, "He insisted on bringing it over himself." A few minutes later the doorbell rang and Barbara answered. She saw Dale standing there with a big smile on his face. Dale noticed that Barbara was still losing weight. Her cheekbones were starting to be visible.

He said, "Here it is, I hope you enjoy it. I'm glad you are interested in this stuff. Applying these things in my life certainly has made a difference." Dale looked over at Frank and said, "Have you been watching your stress tank level?"

Frank, not wanting to fully admit he had been giving some of these things a lot of thought, said in a sarcastic tone, "Oh yeah. All the time."

Dale played along and said, "Good, you can just keep this article. I have another one at home."

Dale turned to leave as Frank said, "Thanks for trying to be so helpful."

"You're certainly welcome," Dale said as he shut the door.

Before Frank and Barbara retired to bed that evening they lay in bed and read the article together.

"STRESS MANAGEMENT TIPS AND PROBLEM SOLVING"

In the fast-paced world we live in, people are trying to speed up the time it takes to do everything. Computers are faster. There are quick lubes, ATM machines, microwaves, and medications that create healing much faster with less side effects. The expectation is that everything should have a quick fix. With the increase in speed that we can perform various tasks, stress also increases. In our society today the expectation is that everything should be done more quickly.

Most people now expect speedier resolutions to problems they are experiencing. Some problems have quick resolutions and others may take days, months, or even years to resolve. There may be times when problems can not be solved immediately and you may need to wait until circumstances permit the problem to be resolved. An example of a problem that may require you to be patient until full resolution can be achieved is an unexpected accident in which your physical and emotional health have been effected. While you are waiting for healing and resolution, you need to have some stress management tools to lower and manage your stress tank level.

The basic idea behind stress management is to find activities you can perform that are healthy, enjoyable or relaxing. When you participate in these activities, your stress tank level will lower and life will be more enjoyable, and you will feel better. Your mind will then be occupied with thoughts that are positive. These positive thoughts will also help your stress tank level stay low.

Keep in mind that your thoughts typically lead to actions. Our thoughts can be managed by practicing positive behaviors, which will in turn create positive thoughts. When thoughts regarding the stressful situation or problem creep in your mind, then refocus your thoughts on what you are currently doing, or what you plan to do to lower your stress level. This may have to be done fairly frequently at first until you can train your mind to stay focused on the positive activities.

QUICK AND LONG TERM STRESS RELIEVERS

Again the key to this is to be aware of your stress tank level. When it starts to rise then utilize one of the long or short term stress relievers.

Quick Stress Relievers

There are many activities that will quickly lower your stress tank level: taking a few deep breaths, taking a hot bath, elevating your legs, taking a break from whatever you are doing, getting your mind focused on the present instead of the past or future, listening to music, watching TV, looking around to find something interesting or beautiful to pay attention to, taking a power nap, meditating, using guided imagery or self hypnosis, doing a hobby, thinking of the blessings in your life, thinking of the problems you have overcome in the past, choosing to see the potential in a situation instead of the pitfalls, focusing on the positives that may result from the problem at hand, and doing something physical that will get you heart pumping. These are all examples of stress relievers.

Long Term Stress Relievers

These are life style and behavioral changes:

Develop an exercise plan. Make sure your top priorities are receiving proper balanced attention. Become proactive instead of reactive. Plan and organize things in your life. Have daily prayer and/or meditation. Develop a hobby or interest. Make it a habit to look for the good or potential in people and situations. Write in a journal the positive and negative experiences. Periodically read over the journal to allow you to see how you resolved past problems. Create a routine of performing service or volunteer work.

Problem Solving Through Stress

Another effective way to deal with stress is to work with it from a problem solving perspective. Many times stress can be the result of a specific problem or many problems. If these problem-solving steps are implemented, stress can be reduced or eliminated.

There are several steps to effectively resolving problems.

First ask yourself this question: Is this problem or issue something I can realistically resolve on my own? If you feel like you can attempt to resolve it on your own, then the below problem-solving steps need to be implemented.

1. Identify the problem. (The problem needs to be specifically defined. For example if the problem is depression, list out all the potential causes and deal with only one of them at a time. You will need to pin down the problem to resolve it effectively. If one of the things that depress you is money, you will need to figure out if it is a spending or budgeting problem.)

2. Identify all potential solutions to the problem.

3. Choose one of these options.

4. Implement it.

5. After implementation, evaluate how well the problem was resolved.

If you feel like the problem is not manageable on your own, then more information or help is needed.

1. Obtain information from the internet, libraries, experts in that subject, books and articles. (Don't rely on just one source.)

2. Ask for another objective opinion on the problem.

3. Go back to the problem and see if you can utilize the problem-solving steps. (You may need to have an expert help you with the problem.)

4. If the problem still can not be resolved, then you will need to move on with your life and periodically come back to see if anything has changed that would allow you to resolve the problem. (Use the short and long term stress management tips while waiting. The goal again during this phase is to watch your stress tank level and implement the stress management tips as needed. Realize that many problems can not be resolved immediately.)

Remember you do not need to allow stress to make you miserable. You have the power and ability to make your life better. Use the problem-solving steps and the quick and long term stress management tools to make your life more fulfilling.

Barbara finished reading the article and said, "This gives us a little more information to work with doesn't it?"

Frank sighed, "Yeah, some more to add to all the rest—lots to think about."

Chapter 7

Timeouts Can Help Change Your Perspective

One beautiful clear morning, Dale called out to Frank, "Let's go to Ma's Café and get something to eat I'm buying." As they waited for their food Frank began to tell Dale about his four-year-old little girl who had been throwing tantrums lately. Frank went on to say that they had been putting her in time out, which had not fully helped. Dale listened intently, and thought he knew just the approach to take.

"Do you put her in time out every time she throws a tantrum?" Dale asked.

Frank responded, "For the most part we do, but sometimes we are so tired we just give her whatever she wants in order to get her to be quiet."

"Well, as you have already discovered," Dale responded, "for your time outs to really work you have to take the time to be consistent using them every time the problem occurs. I remember being in Las Vegas years ago and playing a slot machine. I never won anything. In fact I ended up losing money, but each time I won a little bit of money I had the hope I might win the jackpot. If we believe that there might be one chance of winning a jackpot we may keep playing.

"Children are the same way. Unconsciously, if they know that there might be one chance they can get away with something, then they will keep doing it with the hope that this one time will be their 'jackpot.' If we are consistent at enforcing consequences then it is more likely that our children will discontinue bad behavior."

Trying to heighten Frank's curiosity, Dale continued, "I put myself in time out at times." Frank looked up to see if Dale was joking. Dale continued, "The main reason we put our children in time out is to diffuse an emotionally charged situation and to give them a chance to calm down. Once they are calm, hopefully they can see a new perspective. When I get frustrated I try, but don't always succeed, to have enough self-control to put myself in time out. This can help to achieve the same results for ourselves, as it does for our kids. At any age frustration can create thinking that is very narrow-minded. When we are frustrated or stressed out, we may not think as clearly as we do when we are calm. Many times when we are in an emotionally charged situation, we become more impulsive.

"A while ago I was out tilling, and a rock got stuck in my tiller. I could feel my stress level increasing. My personal opinion is that life is not going to control me, I am going to control my own thoughts and behaviors. I couldn't pry the rock out, so after about a half an hour of prying, I took a break to calm myself down. When I came back to my problem, I was able to see how the rock could be pried out by getting under the tiller. Taking the break reduced my stress, which gave me a new perspective on the problem.

"It is like looking at this pencil. Let's just say that this pencil represents one of our problems. Pretend it is suspended in the air and no one is touching it. How much of the pencil can you see at any one time, even if you get up and walk around the pencil?"

"About half, I guess," said Frank.

"You are right. At any one time, we can see only about half of the pencil. Again, if the pencil represents a problem, and we can see only half of the problem, then we may be able to resolve only half of the problem. When I was on my roof cutting a huge chunk out of it, I could see only half of the problem. The reason is that I was not knowledgeable enough to know the depth of the problem. I didn't want to admit to myself that I didn't have the expertise to resolve this problem adequately. I had to ask some experts to give me more information about what the other side of the problem or pencil looked like. I think many problems that occur in our life are like this. We just need to ask someone what he or she sees on the other side of the pencil.

"The other thing I think is important," Dale further added, "is that we can not effectively problem solve while we are frustrated or upset. Taking a break from a problem may allow us to see a fresh perspective. It's like looking at that pencil that I told you about. If we take a break from the problem, many times when we come back to it we can see the problem from a different angle, which allows us to see a different perspective or point of view. Sometimes this gives us enough new information to effectively resolve the problem."

"It sounds like asking for help is a pretty good way to get rid of a lot of stress," Frank agreed.

"I really think so," Dale said, "It's saved me many times."

"The only problem for me," Frank said, "is that I don't like asking for help, because I think that people expect something in return."

"I think I know who you're talking about," Dale responded. There was a family they both knew who kept tallies on service. "It seems that the family you're referring to really does expect you to help them, if they have helped you. However, I don't think everyone feels that way. Most people help others because they want to. Do you keep track of the people you have helped, and then expect them to return the favor?"

"No, but I know that one family does."

"Yes, but I think they are the exception to the rule."

"It is nice if we can return the favor, when someone helps us, but we can't help everyone all the time." Dale continued, "Keep in mind one thing. We can find that helping someone else can actually make our burdens seem lighter. As you realized when you came over to look at my roof, you were not alone as far as having problems. Also, giving help to someone else can, as we have heard in church, create good feelings inside. Remember, don't help someone if it is going to cause you to be overloaded."

Dale and Frank finished their breakfast. Throughout breakfast Dale marveled at the way Frank was able to handle receiving the information without any sarcasm. He seemed to be reaching out for some help. It felt good for Dale to be back in the role of helping someone work through life's difficulties. However, the pay-off this time was not money.

Chapter 8

Trust, Faith and Patience

Frank, Dale and their families regularly attended the same church every Sunday. One particular Sunday the sermon was about faith, patience, and the growth that comes as a result of trials. This sermon really hit home with Frank. Everything that he had been learning over the last several months just seemed to come together for him.

After church Frank found Dale and excitedly said, "Wow that was a great sermon today wasn't it? That part about adults being like children and how they throw temper tantrums just like children really hit home with me. I really liked it when the preacher said that adults just have more sophisticated versions of tantrums. Instead of throwing ourselves on the floor kicking and screaming, adults give up or engage in self-pity when we don't get our way. I guess the bottom line is the same, we want what we feel we deserve right now. If we don't get it, then we start throwing a temper tantrum, hoping God will see our distress and remove the problem for us. It really helped me to understand that these difficulties we experience end up making us stronger. We may pout, whine, or think 'why me,' but as you have told me, I need to try to see the good that may result from the problems.

"It is awesome to think that if we believe God is all caring and merciful, then we need to trust that there is nothing that we have to suffer alone. Also, we need to know that God will not give us challenges that we can not deal with.

"Today was so great," Frank continued, "I really felt good about what I learned. What hit home for you Dale?"

Dale said, "Well I liked the part about being patient. Frank, how many times have we both said to our kids, when they want something, 'be patient and wait.' God probably gently tells us the same thing, 'Be patient and wait, things will work out.' We just need to have more trust. We desire our children to trust us, and I think God desires us to trust His plan. You know, when we look back at some of the difficulties and problems in our life, we can begin to see more clearly how much faith we expected to make it through the trial. In the sermon today he talked about how we all have natural coping mechanisms. Some of these coping skills are healthy and others are unhealthy. The example of the alcoholic was given. He said that the person who drinks alcohol is using this as a stress management tool. However, this is obviously an unhealthy coping mechanism. We need to find healthy coping skills. After we have been through a stressful event, we can look back and evaluate what coping skills we used and whether they were healthy or unhealthy."

"You know, after today I really feel rejuvenated. I have more confidence and insight into how to resolve my problems," Frank declared.

As they departed that day Dale felt a sense of peace knowing that his friend had gained much needed inner strength. He hoped that he had been part of facilitating the change in his friend.

Chapter 9

The Death of a Loved One

Death has a way of putting things in perspective. One night Frank was awakened by his dear wife's crying out from the pain of a severe headache. Lately she had been having more headaches and pressure in her head. She had been suffering through this pain for several weeks until this one night the pressure became so intense that all she could do was grab her head and scream. Her husband of eighteen years picked her up and gently carried her to the car and drove to the emergency room. She was admitted into the hospital where she received medication to decrease the pain. All the next day various test and procedures were performed. Fearing the worst, they were both very worried and anxious about the results. Late that afternoon when her physician came into her room, he hesitated as looked down at the floor and sighed. "The tests show that you have a brain tumor." They were both devastated. She started to cry, and Frank sat there in shock.

Frank asked, "What does this mean?"

Dr. Montgomery responded, "The tumor is growing extremely fast and is inoperable because of its location. Chemotherapy might help extend life, but I don't know if it is worth the side effects. There is not a whole lot we can do other than help control the pain. I am so sorry."

Barbara was devastated by the news. With tears filling her eyes and her voice quivering, she asked, "How long. . ."

Dr. Montgomery sensed what she was going to ask and gently interjected, "I don't like to tell my patients how long they will live. However, statistically people with this type of rapidly growing tumor will live for several months. If I can do anything for you, let me know. I will check in on you later."

After the physician left the hospital room, they both sat there in silence for what seemed like hours. Barbara, with tears streaming down her face, said to her husband in a soft shaky voice, "Frank I am so scared, I don't want to die. How are we going to tell our kids?"

"I am just not very good at these things," Frank responded. As he continued, he was overcome with emotion and began to cry. Between breaths he said, "I wish I knew what to say and could just make all of this go away."

"Frank, you can't make it go away," she softly exclaimed. "I just need you to be there for me."

Frank sighed and said, "I can't believe that I won't have you anymore."

That evening they gathered their four children together to tell them the bad news. As they revealed the prognosis, little eight-year-old, Krystal, ran over to her mother and said, "Oh mommy please don't die." The two older children sat in shock with tears streaming down their faces.

The youngest, who was five, walked over to her mom with tears in her eyes and said, "Mommy are you going to Heaven?"

Barbara, who was trying to hold back her emotions, between the sobs said, "Yes, Mommy is going to go to Heaven." The mental picture—that mom would not be around anymore—caused everyone to shed more tears.

The next several days were difficult for everyone. There were some periods of uncomfortable silence, though everyone tried to make mom as comfortable as possible.

It was the time of year that the crops now need to be harvested. Frank would have to juggle taking care of his wife along with work on the farm and the housework.

While out working in the field, he found that it helped if he kept his mind occupied with work. This allowed him to avoid the painful feelings surrounding his wife's problem. When he was home he did all he could for the family by cooking, cleaning, and attending to Barbara's needs. Doing these chores also allowed him to avoid these very uncomfortable feelings.

One day Barbara said to her husband, "Frank, you are wearing yourself out. Please slow down and just be with me." Frank stopped folding the laundry and sat down on the bed where his wife lay. He started picking at a callus on his hand.

Tears welled up in his eyes and he groaned as he fell back on the bed, "This is the only way to stop the pain." They talked for the next several hours about some of the great times they had together and some of the difficulties they had overcome. They laughed and cried together. That night turned out to be one of best that they would ever share together.

The next day Frank didn't feel as compelled to hurry out to work on the farm. In fact, he felt more compelled just to stay with his wife. As he was doing some of the necessary chores he found his mind wandering back to the conversation he had shared with his wife the previous evening. Just then he heard a voice. It was Dale. Dale walked over to his friend in the barn and asked, "How are things going, and how is your dear wife?" Frank relayed to him how he had been working like crazy to avoid the painful thoughts and feelings of his wife's inevitable death. He also mentioned to his friend the incredible talk he and his wife had experienced the previous evening.

Dale responded, "It is good you recognized why you were working so much, and the impact it was having. You now have the opportunity to enjoy your wife and love her, knowing that her time is limited. When my son died years ago, I wish I had had the opportunity to say good-bye. Frank, take this opportunity to enjoy your wife and help her pass to the other side. When I heard about your wife having terminal cancer, it reminded me of how precious life is and the need to take a few moments to treasure the little things. We need to pause for a moment and take a mental picture of the special or peaceful times—a hug or kiss from our children, the sounds of nature, and the smell of bacon cooking in the morning, or just stopping for a moment to enjoy a sunset. I used to do much better at enjoying life. Frank, please take advantage of this unique opportunity so you won't regret it later."

"Thanks Dale, you are a good friend. I am going to cut out early today and go home."

Little did Frank know that his friend had arranged to have many of the people from their church come over and finish harvesting his crops.

While Frank was home that afternoon making lunch for his wife, he looked out the window and noticed a crowd gathering in his field. As he watched he saw tractors and trucks. And more people showed up—all people from church. Then they just all started working. He said to his wife, "Come here and look at this." His wife came to the window and was amazed. Barbara wanted to go out there to say thanks, but knew she was too weak to make it by herself, so she asked Frank to help her.

Frank said "Let me just carry you. Her now frail 5' 4" frame only weighed about 90 pounds. It was easy for Frank to carry her. He gently picked her up and walked outside toward the field. Dale and some others met them at the edge of the field.

Tears welled up in everyone's eyes. Frank and Barbara could hardly speak, because of their emotions.

Frank managed to say, "You are a very good friend, Dale, thank you."

Dale responded, "You just enjoy life right now the best you can." Lots of hugs were exchanged and tears shed that day, and everyone involved felt that day was one of the most fulfilling in their lives.

The next several weeks were definitely trying for Frank and his family. Frank was very grateful for his friends and the work they had done on his farm. In fact, each day someone stopped by to do the morning chores. Also, periodically members of their church brought dinners to their home. This was a great blessing to them.

Frank heeded his wife's request to be with her and was grateful for his friend's suggestion to enjoy her. Although it was a difficult time, he took mental pictures of those moments that were most enjoyable and memorable. He had never been closer to his wife. It was a very bittersweet time for him and the kids. They found time to read, tell stories, and play games together. They learned to treasure the brief, good moments.

As the days went by Barbara grew weaker. Finally she sensed death was near. On the night she died, she hugged and kissed each one of her children. She promised she would watch over them from heaven. Barbara and her Frank exchanged words of love. For the next hour they reminisced about the good times. Barbara listened with her eyes closed, and sometime during the course of this conversation, she passed to the other side.

The viewing and funeral were beautiful. After the viewing Dale saw his friend over at his wife's casket. Dale approached

Frank and said, "I still have times when I grieve the loss of my son even though he died four years ago. I read this book on grieving by an expert in the field. She indicates it is normal to have these feelings, and that these feelings may periodically surface throughout my life. That has really helped me."

Frank looked up at his friend and said, "I just can't believe that she is gone." Dale put his hand on Frank's shoulder to try to comfort him. "There is just so much I don't understand. I wish that this were just a bad dream. We all became so close to her before she died and that makes losing her that much more difficult."

Dale responded, "I am going to tell you something that no one except my wife knows. The night before my son died, he and I had an argument about his chores. There are many times that I wished I could live that night over again." Tears fell down Dale's check. "If I could redo the events of that night, I would make sure I talked more calmly to my son and said, 'I love you.' Frank, I know it hurts now, but you and the kids will be so glad you had the opportunity to get so close to Barbara before her death."

A few weeks later, when Frank walked out the front door early in the morning to do his chores, he glanced at the sunrise. Normally he would have just ignored the rising sun and started working, but today he stopped for a few minutes. He sat down on his porch and enjoyed the beautiful array of colors. He recalled what Dale said about enjoying these moments. There was a twinge of pain in his heart, as he wished his wife were here with him. He felt the pain and sadness flooding back like a ton of lead. His initial reaction was to get up and hurry out to the field and start working. Dale's words rang in his ear, telling him that he would continue to grieve over his wife's death and that this would be normal. So he stayed seated. Tears welled up in his eyes. Initially it felt like he would go crazy, but after a few minutes the sadness turned to fondness as he started to remember all the good times he and Barbara had shared together.

Frank learned a good lesson that day. For the first time, He realized that he did not have to spend so much effort trying to keep all of his emotions bottled up. He wished his wife were with him to share in his new insight.

For the first month Frank found himself, at times, in a state of disbelief that she was really gone. While doing the dishes one day he actually called out her name, asking her to bring him a dishtowel. The smell of the shampoo she used or various other sights and sounds would bring back memories, and it would almost seem like she was still living. At times while lying in bed it almost seemed like any minute she would walk through the bedroom door. Often it was difficult to believe she was really dead, and then other times the reality of it would sink so deep that it was almost too much to bear. This roller coaster of thoughts and feelings were beginning to create some strain on him.

One day while he was trying to help his oldest son with an art project, which had always been Barbara's specialty. He became frustrated and said to his son, "I would do anything if she were back with us again." His son nodded and looked down as tears began to form in his eyes. Not knowing how to respond, both just sat in silence for a few minutes. Frank finally said, "Lets just finish this another day." They said good-night to each other and went to bed.

The Worst Day Since his Wife's Death

One morning his little Krystal came to him and said, "I saw mommy last night. She stood at the bottom of my bed and told me that she was happy and she was watching over us. She was wearing this pretty white dress."

Frank quickly blurted out, "Mommy is gone and she is not coming back. You have to just deal with that. That is reality and we are going to have to live with it."

Krystal's long brown hair flew as she took off running to her bedroom crying, "I saw her. Daddy, I know I did."

That day he saw Dale and asked him about the comments his little girl had made. Frank was feeling very guilty about the way he had responded to his daughter. Dale said, "I believe your little Krystal saw your wife. I don't doubt those types of things happen. What did you say to her when she told you this?"

Ashamed, Frank looked down and said, "I got mad at her and told her she wasn't coping very well." Dale sensed that Frank was projecting his own feelings on his daughter and felt it might be beneficial for him to get some help.

He gently said, "Maybe it wouldn't hurt for you to talk to our clergyman about some of these things. He might be able to shed some light on this subject that Krystal has brought up." Not saying anything, Frank quickly changed the subject. He asked Dale how his work was going. They talked a few more minutes and then separated. However, all the rest of that day Frank thought about the possibility of going to talk with his clergyman.

The next day he decided to call and make an appointment to see Gary Robinson, his clergyman. Frank was very ambivalent about seeing him, but made it to the church the day of the appointment. Mr. Robinson greeted him warmly and took Frank back to his office. Frank had never seen the man's office before. It was very warm and inviting. There were pictures of mountains and scenic outdoor views. Instead of sitting behind his desk, as Frank would have thought, the clergyman sat in one of the chairs in front of his desk and invited Frank to sit down in any one of several chairs that were also in front of his desk.

Mr. Robinson started by asking Frank how he and the kids were doing. Frank responded, "That is what I wanted to talk to you about." Frank relayed to Mr. Robinson the emotional roller coaster he was suffering and what his daughter had said several mornings earlier.

The kind man listened intently to Frank and said, "Dealing with the loss of a loved one is one of the most difficult challenges of life. There has been a great deal of research done relating to how people cope with the death of a loved one. There are some typical feelings that many will experience. Kubler Ross, a well know expert in this field, indicated that people may experience denial, anger, depression, bargaining, and then acceptance. You mentioned the time you called out her name, and the disbelief at times that she is gone. This is part of the denial. Being angry with your little girl could be part of this process. You may also be angry at times with your wife for leaving you. You could also feel some anger toward God for taking her from you. This is all normal. When you said to your son that you would do anything to have her back, this is part of the bargaining I mentioned.

"Frank, you may experience these feelings for quite some time. To some degree or another you may have them for the rest of your life. You will eventually get to the acceptance phase and be all right for a while, and then you may experience these stages all over again. You may experience all of the stages in one day. This is all part of grieving. The hope is that the anger and depression are kept in check, and that the intensity of these feeling will decrease, and the interval at which they come will decrease. However, it takes time. Don't let anyone tell you that you should be over it in a certain time frame. Does this make sense to you?"

"Now that you point it out, I can see these stages. But what about my little girl seeing my wife?" Frank asked.

"I don't doubt she saw Barbara, but I am wondering if you are questioning why your wife would come to Krystal and not you?"

"I don't know about that. I just don't know if I believe in that kind of stuff," Frank said.

"Do you believe in life after death?"

"Well yes. But can people from heaven come and visit us?"

"Sometimes children have stronger faith than adults, and that may be why Krystal had this experience. Also, it is possible that your little girl needed to be comforted, and God saw it fit for her to be comforted in this way."

Frank left that day with a new perspective on everything. Although there was still a lot of pain, he found that the things Mr. Robinson told him helped him make sense of everything. He talked to his little Krystal about her experience and found out that there had been two other times that Barbara visited her. Once on the day of the funeral and another night while she was crying herself to sleep. Accepting her statements this time, Frank found comfort in these events.

Frank began forcing himself to slow down to make sure his children were doing all right. It was a challenge at times to slow down his pace, but he noticed he was much calmer and actually just as productive. It was strange not having Barbara around, and he felt some intense periods of loneliness. Before she died, Barbara told him that she wanted him to find another wife that would be a good mother to their children. The thought of this created a real conflict in his mind. He could not imagine himself with anyone else. He had no desire to approach that issue. When Barbara spoke about it to him, he offered no confirmation as to what he would do. He just gently changed the subject. Right now, Frank had no desire to remarry, but in the back of his mind knew that his children needed a mother.

As Frank pondered the occurrences of the last year, he realized how much individual growth he had experienced. It felt good, and he was especially thankful for his friend's help. Without Dale's help, life would have been much more difficult. Dale and Emily had Frank and his children over for dinner a couple of times a month. Dale enjoyed this association. Frank was hoping life would not offer any more major challenges for at least a little while, but by now he knew he was a little more prepared just in case.

Frank loved his children, and wanted to be the best father that he could. He knew that Dale and others would continue to help him. He missed his wife terribly, but somehow he would survive. He knew that the new tools he had gained would help him continue to deal with the future challenges he would face.

Stress Management Tools Discussed in the Book

1. Plan and organize.

2. Wake up on time each day.

3. Eat a proper diet and exercise.

4. Don't allow your thoughts to make the worst out of a situation.

5. Find the good out of a bad situation.

6. Be proactive not reactive.

7. Focus on your accomplishments, not your failures. (Take time to review your accomplishments.)

8. Be an optimist not a pessimist. (Learn from the past but don't dwell on it.)

9. Don't overdo and overload yourself with too much.

10. Find time to relax and enjoy your surroundings.

11. Get in touch with the present through your five senses.

12. Acknowledge the bad but don't dwell on it and allow it to consume you.

13. Take breaks throughout the day.

14. Take a couple of deep breaths.

15. Put your self in time out if you get too stressed.

16. Find something to look forward to on a daily, weekly, monthly, and yearly basis.

17. Find a hobby or activity you enjoy and do it (especially during stressful events).

18. Find new things each day you are thankful for.

19. Realize that time does heal wounds (emotional and physical).

20. Study the Serenity Prayer. (Know where you have control and where you do not.)

21. Realize that 99 percent of our worries never happen.

22. Have a strategy to deal with that 1 percent.

23. Realize you always have choices.

24. Pray. (Be thankful and ask for help.)

25. Ask for help from family, friends, and neighbors if needed.

26. Accept help when offered.

27. Do something productive or fun that is healthy to help get your mind off the stress.

28. Use the problem-solving model.

29. Obtain as much information as you can about the problem, before you decide a course of action (Don't make major decision with your stress tank overflowing.)

30. Don't make decisions when your stress tank is near the top.

31. Always monitor your stress tank level. Know the signs and symptoms that indicate it is rising, and know which activities can lower it.

32. Know which long and short-term stress relievers benefit you.

33. Talk about the stress with an expert or another person to gain their perspective.

34. Don't expect someone else to solve your problem.

35. Give your mind a break from the problem.

36. Find Balance in your life. (Review the six areas.)

37. Have patience and trust in God or your higher power.

38. Learn self control.

39. Analyze the way you have resolved past difficulties and use those strategies that have been successful with your current problem.

40. See the problem as opportunity for growth.

41. Do something to help another in need.

42. Learn from your own mistakes and mistakes of others.

ABOUT THE AUTHOR

Stephen S. Havertz has a Master of Social Work Degree from the University of Nevada Las Vegas and a Bachelor of Arts degree from Weber State University. He is a Licensed Clinical Social Worker and has been doing various types of counseling in the mental health arena since 1988. He has worked in various in-patient and out-patient clinics during his career. Currently he is the Manager of Clinical Services for the company where he is employed.

He has specialized in the treatment of various mood disorders and stress and anxiety disorders. He is also specialized in utilizing various relaxation techniques with his clients. He commonly teaches clients how to use guided imagery, self-hypnosis, and meditative techniques to create healing and relaxation in their lives.

Stephen for years has enjoyed public speaking. His audiences have enjoyed the fun stories he shares and his well-organized and easy-to-understand concepts. Powerful metaphors drive his points into the hearts of his listeners. Individuals leave his seminars with strong motivation to make positive changes in their lives.

Weaving these stress management principles into this story has been in the development made for many years. He originally began writing a book with just these concepts without the story. The idea to present two different individual styles of dealing with stress came to him one day when watching a video. It became clear that readers would gain much more from actually seeing how these principles were used in contrast to just reading about the concepts.

Stephen has been happily married to his wife Camille for thirteen years and they have three children together. They currently reside in Layton, Utah.

Stephen enjoys spending time with his wife and children. One of their favorite vacations has been going to Disneyland. He also enjoys various sports and outdoor activities.

Stephen is available for speaking engagements. Please contact him at <u>cshavertz@juno.com</u>

CEDAR FORT, INCORPORATED
Order Form

Name:_____

Address: _____

City: _____ State: _____ Zip: _____

Phone: ( ) _____ Daytime phone: ( ) _____

The Farmer and Dale

Quantity: _____ @ $7.95 each: _____

plus $3.49 shipping & handling for the first book: _____

(add 99¢ shipping for each additional book)

Utah residents add 6.25% for state sales tax: _____

TOTAL: _____

Mail this form and payment to:

Cedar Fort, Inc.

925 North Main St.

Springville, UT 84663

You can also order on our website **www.cedarfort.com**

or e-mail us at sales@cedarfort.com or call 1-800-SKYBOOK

9 26575 75910 8